Buzz the Bee

Written by:

Kevin MacKenzie

Illustrated by:

Adrian Nottage and Kevin MacKenzie

For Ophelia and Esmé

May your imaginations and creativity inspire others

the same way you inspired me and this book.

I love you both very much.

Love,

Dad

This is Buzz.

Buzz is a bee who lives in a beehive next to a big blue house, below a window, on a branch in a bright green bush.
He lives there with all his bee friends. But Buzz is not your typical bee. Buzz is a bee who bee-lieves he can be anything he wants to be.

One day Buzz and his friends were making honey when Buzz suddenly stopped and asked, "Why do we have to make honey every day? There's got to be something else to do besides make honey." All of the other bees stopped, looked up and started to laugh. "Something else besides make honey?"

"Buzz…
Bees.
Make.
Honey."

"It's what we do. We make honey," they said, as they went back to work. But Buzz thought a little harder.

"Why does that have to be the only thing bees do? I like making honey, but I want to try something else. I want to be more than just a bee who makes honey."

The other bees stopped and looked up again. "Buzz, you're a bee. Just a little bee. What do you think you can do?"

"I don't know," Buzz said. "Any… anything I want. Great things! Big things! Adventurous things! I want to…" Buzz was interrupted by the grumblings of the Big Big Man who lived in the big blue house next to the bright green bush and their beehive.

All the bees were afraid of the Big Big Man because, well, he was really big and they were pretty sure he didn't like bees. As they looked out of the hive they saw the Big Big Man with his hands around a huge rock on the ground.

"IT! WON'T! BUDGE!"

he said, before giving up and sitting on the grass.

Buzz thought for a moment before yelling out loud, "That's it!"

All the other bees turned around. "What's it?"

"What I'm going to do!" Buzz said excitedly. "I'm going to help the Big Big Man move that huge rock."

The bees almost fell over with laughter. "You? A tiny little bee? Move that huge rock? Hahaha! He'll swat you before you can even try."

"Well…at least I'm going to try," Buzz said.
"I may be little, but I have big dreams and
I'm going to follow them." Buzz turned
around and quickly flew out of the hive.
"Buzz, wait!" all the other bees yelled.
But it was too late. He was
already gone.

Before Buzz could even realize what he
had just decided to do, he was face-to-face
with the Big Big Man.

"AHHHHH!"

Buzz yelled, before flying to the closest flower.

"Come on Buzz," he said to himself. "You can do it.

Don't be afraid. This is your chance."

He took a deep breath, buzzed his wings

and flew toward the Big Big Man and the huge rock.

BZZZZZZZZZ!

Buzz flew right by the Big Big Man's nose.

BZZZZZZZZZ!

Buzz flew right by the Big Big Man's ear.

WHOOOOOSH!

The Big Big Man swiped his huge hand, just missing Buzz.

"That was close," Buzz thought, but he wasn't about to give up. He flew as fast as he could.

He loop-de-looped.

He zigged.

He zagged.

And finally landed right on the huge rock.

All the other bees still watching from the hive cheered.

"Buzz made it! He made it!"

Not really sure what to do next,

Buzz gripped the rock with his little bee feet

and buzzed his wings with all his bee strength.

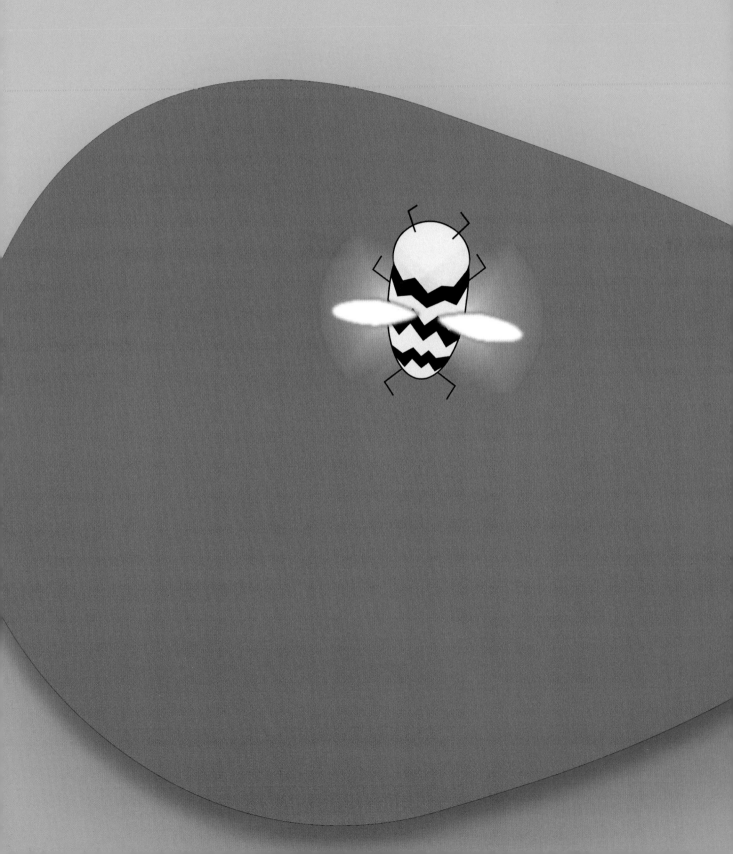

Bzzzzzzzzzzzzz!

The Big Big Man looked down to see what
all the commotion was about and saw Buzz,
buzzing as fast as he could.
"What is this bee doing?" he thought.

The Big Big Man lifted up his huge huge boot

and was about to…

but he stopped.

"Wait a second.

"Wait. A. Second.

Well I'll be," said the Big Big Man.

"I can't believe it.

This little bee is trying to help me."

When he looked even closer, he saw the

bravest little bee using everything he had

to move a rock one thousand times his size.

"I see it, but I don't believe it." said the Big Big

Man. "But hold on, little bee, I'm coming."

One last time, the Big Big Man wrapped his arms around the rock. Buzz was scared, but he wasn't going to quit.

The Big Big man yelled, "Here we go lil' bee!

One!
Two!
Three!"

And together they lifted with all their strength. At first nothing happened, but slowly, and amazingly, the rock began to move. "Keep going!" groaned the Big Big Man. "Almost there!" as he and Buzz, with one last push, flipped the huge rock over and watched it roll down the hill.

The Big Big Man cheered as he looked around
for his new friend so he could thank him,
but Buzz was so tired he fell to the ground
and was lying exhausted in the grass.

The Big Big Man quickly spotted him.
"There you are, little bee," as he reached down
and gently placed him in the palm of his hand.
The other bees were still nervously watching
from the hive,

but the Big Big Man would never hurt this little bee who just did the impossible.

He just gently held Buzz in his hand, looked down at him and said, "Well, look at you, little bee. Without your help, I would've never been able to move that huge rock. You may just be a little bee, but you have the biggest heart I've ever seen."

The Big Big Man walked toward the big blue house next to the bright green bush and gently placed Buzz back in the hive.

The other bees held him up and cheered.

"Hip hip hooray!

Buzz! The smallest bee with the biggest heart!"

Then they apologized for not believing in their friend.

Buzz just smiled, tired and happy to be home.

Happy to finally be the bee he knew he could be.

A bee that could be more
than just a bee who made honey.

A bee who can be anything he wants to be.

The End